THE TALE OF
Three
Brothers

THE TALE OF Three Brothers

VIKTOR ZUBIN

The Tale of Three Brothers

Copyright © 2024 by Viktor Zubin. All rights reserved.

No part of this publication may be reproduced, stored in a retrieval system or transmitted in any way by any means, electronic, mechanical, photocopy, recording or otherwise without the prior permission of the author except as provided by USA copyright law.

This novel is a work of fiction. Names, descriptions, entities, and incidents included in the story are products of the author's imagination. Any resemblance to actual persons, events, and entities is entirely coincidental.

The opinions expressed by the author are not necessarily those of URLink Print and Media.

1603 Capitol Ave., Suite 310 Cheyenne, Wyoming USA 82001
1-888-980-6523 | admin@urlinkpublishing.com

URLink Print and Media is committed to excellence in the publishing industry.

Book design copyright © 2024 by URLink Print and Media. All rights reserved.

Published in the United States of America
ISBN 978-1-68486-677-9 (Paperback)
ISBN 978-1-68486-678-6 (Digital)

16.08.23

Inspired by: A Russian song called, "The Ballad of the Three Sons". However, some elements were altered for dramatic effect and the potential for continuation of the story. With that said, the core elements and theme will remain the same

Contents

Chapter 1: The Mountain King 1
Chapter 2: The Trial of the Three Brothers 3
Chapter 3: Elliot 5
Chapter 4: Exams and Hellish Training 8
Chapter 5: Orphan 14
Chapter 6: The Barbarian Attack 16
Chapter 7: Mars – The Greatsword Wielder 19
Chapter 8: Elliot – the Hero 22
Chapter 9: Heartbreak 25
Chapter 10: The Runaway 29
Chapter 11: Leo – The Master Merchant 31
Chapter 12: Alejandro – The Commoner 34
Epilogue 37
Afterword 39

CHAPTER 1

The Mountain King

Once upon a time, there lived a king. The king was beloved by all: The clergy, the nobility and the common folk. He did his very best to keep the interest of the people at heart. The king was nicknamed, "The Mountain King". The king was not a big fan of his nickname, but he gave up after a while.

The reason behind the king's nickname was the region that he ruled. The castle was basically surrounded by mountains. You could always hear an echo late at night. Thankfully, the parts where there were no mountains were a valley, multiple valleys in fact. Furthermore, the valleys were separated from the mountains by a river that flowed right down the middle.

Because of the geographically strategic location of the castle, not only did the castle look like an impenetrable fortress, but the river that flowed down the middle was used to turn the valleys into fertile farmland.

The king had three sons: the firstborn – Elliot, a man of physical prowess and strength. When it came to brute strength there was no one to match him. Because of this, he became prideful and set his sights on the throne, expecting to be the next king after his father's death. Most of all, he desired to make his father proud by accomplishing great feats.

The second son – Leo, a man of a lean build. Not as physically strong as Elliot, but strong enough to defend himself. However, what he lacked in muscle, he made up for in brain. Leo and Elliot were constantly competing with one-another. Because of this, Leo developed a stubborn attitude. He learned to never give up, no matter the cost.

The third son – Alejandro, the weakest of them all in terms of brute strength. He was not as smart as his brother Leo. However, Alejandro took to heart everything his father taught him [and his brothers]. He became a man of a humble heart, just like his father, the king. He had no intention of succeeding the throne, for he realized early on, that it was a pointless endeavor.

CHAPTER 2

The Trial of the Three Brothers

When all three brothers turned 15 years old, the king threw a party to celebrate his sons' birthdays. "Today, Elliot, Leo and Alejandro, officially became adults!", the king exclaimed.

Everyone was invited to the party. The clergy, the nobleman and the common folk, all awaited the announcement of the heir to the throne. Many expected Elliot to be named heir, not only because he was the eldest son, but also Elliot was the strongest out of all of them.

The king continued, "I have decided to name an heir! However, each of my sons will have to pass a trial to become king. All three of you wanted to see the outside world, and here is your chance. You are all adults now and are free to make your own decisions in life. What road you walk in life is up to you. However, I implore you: DO NOT forget what I have taught you all. Do not forget about: love, humility, kindness, forgiveness, and generosity." DO NOT forget these virtues of life as you forge your own road in life! That is my trial to all of you!"

"We will not forget!", all three exclaimed in unison.

"Good", said the king "as far as I know, there is a town just down these mountains. I suggest you start there. Although it pains me to see you go, I bid you farewell. May my prayers keep you from harm"

After the announcement, everybody broke into a commotion. The populace did not expect such a result. The king raised his palm in the air, and waited for everyone to calm down. Soon everyone calmed down and waited patiently for the king to explain himself. "I know that many of you did not expect such a result. Many of you were hoping that Elliot, my eldest son, would inherit the throne. However, I want the next king to be a man of virtue and be determined solely based on hierarchy, hence the trial." After hearing such an explanation, many were still confused. However, they had no say in the matter because the word of the king was law. And so, begins the journey of the three brothers as they head out into the outside world.

CHAPTER 3

Elliot

Disclaimer: This chapter is from Elliot's point of view

Down the mountains, there stood a town. This town was nicknamed, "The town of Beginnings" because most of the people there were as young as 15 years old [15 years old is the age of adulthood], who are trying to make a name for themselves.

The town itself consisted of four major districts: The Holy Church District, the Noble/Business District, the Military District and the Commoner District.

The Holy Church District – a place where most of the clergy resided. In the middle of the district, there stood a large church where people gathered for weekly sermons and donations. The church bell was often used in times of emergencies.

The Noble/Business District – a place where people could be trained to become Merchants. Also, everything you wish to buy or sell was located in the Noble District. Many of the noblemen had villas here. People who seek wealth and connections, make the Noble District their base of operations. Finally, most people who can't afford a villa, but still want to stay at a comfortable Inn, choose the Noble District.

The Military District – a place where only the strong gather, but not many survive. Military training academy is the central building of this District. Here you are trained in everything, but can you survive it?

Finally, the Commoner District – a place where the common folk live. They have the worst living conditions and are often mistreated. This is due to the fact that commoners have no social standing in society. It is not uncommon to see beggars and cripples in the Commoner District.

After all the Districts came a villa, largest in town. In that villa the King of the town, Arthur, with his beautiful Queen Guenavire and three daughters: the eldest, Athena. After her, Sobrina, and finally, Rose.

"Finally! Now I can prove to my father, the King, that only I am worthy of succeeding him as the next King!". With that declaration, I climbed down the mountains and entered the town known as "The Town of Beginnings".

The town itself was surrounded by a wooden wall with four archer towers at each of the corners along with two archers at each of the archer towers. Overall, the town was weak defense wise.

When I entered the "Town of Beginnings", the first thing I noticed was the three Districts: Church, Noble/Business and Military. The Church and the Noble Districts at least looked the part. The Church District had a big building in the middle of it that looked like a church, with a golden cross (I guess that's where the District gets its name).

Next came the Noble District – everybody yelling at each other, trying to sell their wares to the newcomers like me. Although many offered me many things as I walked by, I went past them, uninterested.

After that came the Military District. The Military District captivated me the most. In the center stood a building similar to a school but with a unique style. The symbol of the academy was a circle with: a sword on top, a shield on the bottom, a bow to the left and a spear to the right. That is the first thing I saw when I entered the Military District. There were two guards standing at the entrance to the academy. They were wearing silver armor with helmets, a sword at the hip and a spear in hand.

"Excuse me, how do I enroll here? I am new here!". I called out.

"Ah, newbie! Welcome to the Town of Beginnings". One of the guards answered.

"Thank you!"

"What is your name?"

"My name is Elliot; I wish to enroll into the Military academy!"

"If you want to enroll, then you have to pass a few tests!"

"What tests?"

"If you want to find out, go talk to our commander in charge!"

"Thanks, I will!"

"Good luck, you're gonna need it!"

"Where is the commander?"

"See the house next to the Military academy? He's right there"

"Thanks"

"You're welcome"

And so, my adventure has begun.

CHAPTER 4

Exams and Hellish Training

Disclaimer: This chapter is from Elliot's point of view

"Welcome new recruits! If you are standing here today, that means you have passed all your tests and drills to join the military academy. However, do not become complacent. Your training will only get harder from here on out. Remember, no mercy, kill the enemy!"

"ROAR!", the whole battalion exploded in a battle cry. The one giving the speech was Mark, our second-in-command. Also, he is the one who supervised my tests. After the tests were over, he said, "You have potential kid." then left. Now all that training feels years ago! However, the memory of it sends shivers down my spine.

After talking with the guard, I walked right across to the old house and knocked on the front door. *Knock Knock*

"Who is it? common in!"

I did as I was told and closed the door behind me. What I saw shocked me! Right there, in the living room sat a guy as old as my father. I could tell that he was an experienced warrior. He was sitting in an arms chair looking at me from head to toe. Appearance wise he was a well-built man. You could see his muscles through his white t-shirt. I could tell did his fair-share of training.

"Hello Mr., are you the commander of the army?"

"Depends on who's asking."

"Forgive me for my late introduction, my name is Elliot, son of the Mountain King."

"The Mountain King?"

"You knew my father?"

"Well, I guess you could say that. We used to be brothers-in-arms, your father and I, we fought many battles together against the Barbarians. Each Spring they would attack our town to get supplies for the Winter. Ah, those were the days! After another victory against the Barbarians, your father said that he was too old for all this fighting and violence. He took his men along with his wife, who was constantly waiting for us to return from the battlefield, and built the castle in the mountains away from civilization."

"That's weird. Father never talked about his past, I wonder why?"

"After our final battle together as brothers of the sword, your father changed. He started spouting nonsense about: kindness, forgiveness, generosity and love. To think that he used to be the greatest warrior the world has ever seen. He graduated from the Military academy with honors too. Such a shame. What's your name again, son?"

"Elliot, sir!"

"What can I do for you Elliot?"

"I would like to enroll in the Military Academy sir. I was told that I need to pass some tests to enroll."

"Come here, let me get a closer look at you." I did as I was told. The commander looked at me up closely, spun me around three times and exclaimed, "Marvelous! Broad shoulders, strong back, you are a reflection of your father! Come with me I will introduce you to someone. The name's Mars by the way. Nice to meet ya kid."

"The pleasure's mine, Mr. Mars."

"Just Mars is fine, I am not *that* old, am I?"

"No! Of course, not sir!"

"Good, now let's go."

When Mars and I had gone through the front gate of the Military Academy. Everyone was gazing at us. I found out later that many of the knights highly respected Mars, so everyone was looking at him with admiration.

The Academy layout itself was unique. There were many buildings that correspond to what you would learn in that building. There were buildings with the symbol of: a sword, bow & arrow, horse [to learn horseback riding], spear and finally, shield. Many Knights chose only one weapon to focus on along with horseback riding. Besides the buildings of the main disciplines there was one building with the symbol of a horse shoe where horses would breed. Finally, there was an open field where sparring matches between knights would occur, while the rest would place bets on who would win. The open field was only used for sparring, when everyone was done with their training for the day.

I was amazed by everything. You could hear the stomping of hooves and the whistling of arrows hitting their mark. It was amazing! I was so mesmerized by the scenery, that I didn't notice how we made it to a building in the far left-hand corner that looked like a tavern. When we entered the tavern, the first thing I saw was a girl around my age, with short brown hair, brown eyes, a baby face, and a nice figure.

"Lucy, is Mark here?"

"Oh, Commander, sorry I didn't see you there! Yes, Mark is upstairs.

"Thanks, allow me to introduce Elliot, I have high hopes for this kid."

"Hello Elliot, nice to meet you, my name's Lucy."

"The pleasure's all mine" I said, then I took her hand and kissed it slightly while looking in her eyes. She blushed slightly. I added, "Lucy, has anyone ever told you that you are the most beautiful woman I have ever laid eyes on?". I hit the nail on the head because as soon as I said that, her face became as red as a tomato and she covered her face with her hands and ran off. I, meanwhile, stood there with a grin on my face.

"So, you're a lady killer too ha! Just like your father used to be."

As we climbed the stairs to the second floor, I noticed that the tavern had around ten tables plus the counter. When we got to the farthest door, Mars knocked on the door.

"Common in!"

"Hey Mark, I've got a new recruit for you. He's got a lot of potential. Will you train him for me?"

"Is that a personal favor, Mars?"

"Of course, it is. I will owe you one"

"You bet. What is the name of the recruit?"

"Elliot. What disciplines does he want to learn"

"I would like to learn: swordplay, spearman ship, horseback riding and shield wielding."

"Alright Elliot, because it was a favor from Mars, I registered you personally. Training starts at the crack of dawn. You sleep in the Swordplay Barracks. Good Luck, you will need it more than you know.

Next morning at daybreak, "Get up you lazy mutts! It's time for your sword training. 1,000 sword swings use the wooden swords for now. After that, put on your leather armor, take a wooden sword and run ten laps. Run like your life depends on it. With each day that passes we will add more weight to everything. Finally, pick anyone who's left after the first two drills and spar with them until one of you gives up. Now go!". After I did 1,000 swings my hands were sore and numb. The ten laps seemed easy, but I could barely hold my sword in hand. My hands and feet were numb now. I don't know how I did it, but there was one more knight left standing. For me, this was not training, it was real. If I was this tired in a real battle, how would I fight? Fight with intuition and instincts. All I had to do was get my sword to his neck before he gets to me, *NOW!* As his sword was coming to get me, I dodged reflexively, pointed my wooden sword at the knight and murmured, "You're dead! I won!" Before collapsing to the ground, out of exhaustion.

"Man, the kid is good! Mars wasn't lying! He's got a good build with broad shoulders. Good reflexes with killer instincts. A little bit of polishing, and he will become a monster, perhaps rivaling Mars when was young"

The next day, the same thing happened with the spear training. 1,000 spear throws and thrusts. Then ten laps with leather armor and hold the spear. Finally, spear sparring. I passed out a second time because of exhaustion [giving it my all].

The day after that, shield training: 1,000 shield bashes, ten laps with a shield and a dagger. Finally, Shield sparring, first to be knocked down loses. If you are laying on the ground, you are as good as dead. Last on the agenda was horseback riding. Build a relationship with the horses. Then ride ten laps to get comfortable. Finally, pick a wooden weapon and ride with that weapon on the horse. I chose to alternate between weapons to be a well-balanced warrior.

Before I knew it, one year had passed.

"Well Elliot, I guess it's that time of the year again ha. Fresh batch of recruits. Seems like only yesterday that you were brought as a new recruit."

"Please don't remind me! I barely survived that hell. I still get nightmares!"

"Quit whining, you big baby! Look how strong you have become, and that's only after a year! You become more terrifying by the day."

"I will take that as a compliment."

"Common let's get start—" Before Mark could finish, the Church bell rang in an emergency.

"We are under attack! Barbarians are attacking!"

"Not them again" said Mark, "How many of them!" he called out to the archer on the archer tower.

"Four hundred strong. Among them: 100 slingers. 100 calvary and 200 infantries."

"This is bad! 200 of us are veterans with talent. The other 200 are new recruits! No matter. Prepare for defense!"

"Wait! There is a Giant coming from the back! He appears to be carrying a club"

"What! Don't tell me that the Barbarians have struck an alliance with the Giants clan, if they did then we are doomed"

CHAPTER 5

Orphan

Disclaimer: Lucy's point of view

I grew up in the Commoner District of the Town of Beginnings. My parents and I were extremely poor, but somehow, we made it work. The Commoner District was filled with poor people, beggars and cripples. Many of them became sick frequently and fast. When I was 10 years old, I lost my parents to a severe cold. They told me to stay away, so that I wouldn't catch the cold. After they passed on, I was forced to fend for myself.

One day, when I got caught stealing because I was hungry [out of inexperience of being a thief], the merchant threatened to sell me into slavery, since I didn't have a guardian to look after me.

However, at that moment I was saved, saved by the commander of the knights. The second-greatest warrior of his generation. He took me in as his daughter and put me to work in the Military District tavern. Perhaps he thought I was cute enough to work as a waitress.

I got used to my new job fairly quickly. Before I knew it, years had passed. I am 14 now. Many of the men who visited the tavern started whistling in my direction. I thought that they were drunk and they didn't mean it.

I had one guy tell me, "Boy am I jealous of the guy who marries you". That's when I realized they were serious. That's when it happened, I was working as usual then a drunk knight stopped me from leaving his table, set me on his lap and tried to kiss me! I was terrified! Thankfully Mars saved me once again.

Then one day, when the tavern was still empty, Mars walked in with a young man my age. I was mesmerized by him.

However, to not let it show, I pretended to look at paperwork. "Lucy, you there?"

"Oh Commander, sorry didn't see you there"

"That's alright. I would like to introduce you to Elliot one of our potential new recruits"

"Hello Elliot. My name's Lucy, Nice to meet you" I said. Up close he was even more handsome than I thought.

"The pleasure is all mine".

Then he did something I didn't expect. He grabbed my hand gently and kissed it lightly. I felt my cheeks burning red. However, what he did next shocked me to the core. He looked straight into my eyes and said, "You are the most beautiful woman I have ever laid my eyes on". When he said that I couldn't hold it any more. My whole face became crimson red. Then Mars added, "So? You are a lady killer too huh? Just like your father used to be."

After that, I ran away into my room. My heart couldn't stop pounding. I said to myself, "Am I in love?" If I had known then that my pounding heart would be heartbroken, I wouldn't have been so excited.

CHAPTER 6

The Barbarian Attack

In a land far, far, away from the Town of Beginnings, there stood a Barbarian village celebrating a wedding of the son of the village chief. "Congratulations! May you live long and prosper!"

Meanwhile, the fathers of the bride and groom were talking among themselves, "You have no idea how much my son loves your daughter. I have never seen him so happy in his life. This brings back memories of how I married his mother, oh those were the days"

"You are getting old, my friend. I am glad that our arrangement came to fruition. However, I do have a concern. Our food supplies are dwindling. Now that we combined both our villages, we need twice the food. When are we going to raid the Town of Beginnings?"

"Soon, I have just signed a peace treaty with the Giants clan. They have agreed to let us take one Giant to the raid. I don't want to lose my men needlessly like I have done in the past. That damned commander with his greatsword and the so-called Mountain King. The Giants have asked us to bring as many females as possible. It is the mating season for the Giants soon. Gather as many men as possible. We set out to raid the day after tomorrow. How many men can we gather at that time?"

"Around 400 strong."

"Make sure that the men going to raid all have children. Those who are childless are forbidden to go raid."

"Yes chief"

Two days later. "Is everyone ready? To Battle!"

When the Church bell rang in an emergency, the King of the Town of Beginnings gathered his three daughters and said to them, "Athena, Subrina, Rose listens to me! Should the town fall into ruin I want you to use the secret passageway to escape. Your survival is the most important to me. Be smart, escape on time. Otherwise, you will be taken prisoner and most likely raped. Please if such a fate befalls you. Kill yourselves. Each of you has a dagger up your sleeves. Use it if necessary."

"Yes father!" all three said in unison. Meanwhile, Rose, the youngest of the three said to herself, *yea right! I am ditching this place at the first sign of danger. I have no chances of becoming queen anyway.*

The clashing of swords could be heard everywhere, along with the groaning of wounded knights. Both sides were at a stalemate for what seemed like the longest of times. Then the sounds of footsteps could be heard across the battlefield.

Stomp! Stomp! Stomp! Stomp! "The Giant is coming!". A short distance away from the battlefield, the silhouette of a Giant could be seen from far away. Standing at 10ft tall holding a club the size of a human body. Wearing armor specifically tailored for the Giants. The armor itself was extremely heavy for the regular human. A regular human would be crushed in an instant.

Elliot, the eldest of the sons of the Mountain King, has killed the most Barbarians out of all the knights that are present in the battlefield. *Where did the Giant come from? I have to distract him until Mars and Mark get here.* "Hey ugly get over here!". I threw the spear that I had on me, just like I have been trained. The spear hit a bullseye. "ROAR! That hurts, you puny humans! I will crush you! All of you!". Once I had his attention as fast as I could and picked up another spear off of a dead knight. All this running with armor and weapons brought flashbacks of daily training. *Run! Run! Run! Don't Stop!*

Thankfully the Giant was slow, so I was able to kite him and throw spears at him at regular intervals, buying everyone more time.

The first one to arrive on the battlefield was Mark. I could tell that he has already battled a few Barbarians on his way here. "Hey Elliot, how are you holding up?"

"Mark, what took you guys so long? I am already at mylimit!"

"Calm down soldier, keep a cool mind. Mars will show up shortly. Let's keep this Giant busy until Mars shows up! The rest of you keep the slingers away from us!"

"Sir, yes sir!"

Mark has never taken spearman ship training, but he was good with the sword. "I will tank, you throw spears!" "Alright! With that, Mark attacked the Giant in a melee battle.

Clash! Thud! Thud! Clash! Thud! "He's too sturdy, my sword barely grazed him" At that moment a slingers' rock flew in our direction. I was able to dodge it, but Mark was too focused on the Giant to notice.

Thump! "Hey, I thought I told you guys to keep the slingers off us! Useless!" That moment is all it took for Mark to be distracted. When he focused back on the Giant, the club was already in full swing. Mark tried to block with the sword but that was not enough. When the club connected, every bone in Mark's body was crushed. He died instantly.

"Maaaaaaaaark!"

The Giant roared in victory

CHAPTER 7

Mars
The Greatsword Wielder

"Mark! Are you alright? No common man, talk to meeeee! (sobbing). I will kill you if it's the last thing I do! (To the Giant)". I picked up a spear from another dead knight and threw it towards the Giant. Because of the Giant, the stalemate was broken. Screams could be heard everywhere. The Barbarians were killing men on sight. However, for some reason, they did not kill the women. Instead, all the women were taken as prisoners. Whatever the Barbarians were planning to do to them cannot be good.

Many of our goods were stolen as well. The morale of the knights has started to dwindle. At that moment Mars appeared on the battlefield. He showed up wearing his armor and carrying the largest great sword I have ever seen.

Because of the spear that I threw, the Giant became enraged and chased after me. I kept picking up spears of my dead comrades and throwing them at the Giant. However, the Giant was big and it had armor. Even though it was wounded from all my spears, it seemed as though he was unharmed.

Then Mars came up to me and said, "Step aside boy, I got this!" Then he came up to the Giant and in practiced motion made an X on the Giants' chest. Not only were the Giant wounded but the great sword cut through the armor. ROAR! The Giant cried in agony. It no longer paid any attention to me. It focused on Mars.

Meanwhile, the Barbarians kept stealing whatever supplies they could. The Slingers saw that the Giant was struggling. Therefore, they supported him even more by throwing rocks at Mars using their slingshots. When I saw that, I tried to help by removing the slingers.

However, there were too many of them. Under the rock barrage Mars's movements have slowed down considerably. Even though Mars could still parry the Giants' club, It was not enough. The Giant was too quick. The club came down hard. Mars was swatted away like a fly. As he flew, he hit a nearby tree. I ran up to him to see if he was ok. His back was hunched over against the tree. He was coughing blood, "Mars are you alright? I don't understand how you could lose!"

"Everyone gets old kid. Why do you think you found me in that house right next to the academy? I felt I was getting too old for this shit. My age has finally caught up to me. I can't save them anymore kid. You have to save them. Use my great sword". With that, Mars drew his last breath and died from his injuries.

First, I sob uncontrollably. My father figure was murdered in front of me. Then with new found determination, I kept picking up new spears from my dead comrades.

The Giant realized that Mars is dead and switched his target to me. With spears within reaching distance, I threw each of them. This time I was aiming for the eyes. The wounds from my spear-throwing, plus the double cross slash finally took its toll. The Giant slowed down considerably.

Because of this, I was able to aim at the eyes quite comfortably. ROAR! *Bullseye!* The Giant dropped his club to cover his pierced eye. ROAR! *There goes the second one!* With both eyes gone, the Giant didn't know where he was going. He covered both his eyes with his hands and roared in pain. Blood coming out of both eyes!

Because the Giant didn't know where he was going, he tripped on the many rocks left by the slingers. He fell on this with a thud. I dragged the greatsword along the ground and with all the strength I could muster, I swung the greatsword for the first time chopping the head of the Giant in the process.

"Victory is mine!" I screamed. Then I laughed. Then I sobbed uncontrollably.

CHAPTER 8

Elliot
the Hero

Once the knights saw that the Giant was dead, they cheered uncontrollably. They picked me up, armor and all, started throwing me up into the air and saying, "Hip hip hooray! Elliot – the Hero has saved this town from complete and utter destruction! We should make a statue of Elliot depicting his great achievement!"

Under all the excitement, the crowd started preparing for the construction of the statue of Elliot – the Hero. At this moment the King of the Town of Beginnings has made a grand appearance. He was dressed in a flashy attire: red cape, golden garments and a crown upon his head.

Everyone who saw him approaching stepped out of the way. He was escorted by the Royal Guards: The elite of elites.

They surrounded the King in a square formation

"It is nice to meet you, young man. What is your name and who is your father?"

I kneeled in front of the King and answered, "My name is Elliot, son of the Mountain King Your Majesty!"

"Mountain King? You are his son? It is no wonder that you killed the Giant wish such ease"

"With all due respect Your Majesty, I did not defeat the Giant on my own. I have had the assistance of Mark – the second in command and Mars – the Greatsword Wielder."

"Oh? Where are they?"

"Both perished in battle sire"

"Oh Heavens! How truly unfortunate!"

"If I may be so bold your Majesty, I have a request."

"What is your request? You may speak freely."

"I request for Mark and Mars to be buried with honors sire, if possible"

"Of course, it is possible! Gilbert!"

Gilbert was a leader of the Royal Guards. He was fairly muscular and a close friend of the King. You could tell that he was a veteran with a lot of battle experience. He was wearing the same golden armor, only his helmet was different. The helmet that Gilbert wore had three feathers on the back.

"Yes sir?"

"Make sure that Mark and Mars are buried with all the honors of the veteran knights, Go!"

"Your will is my command."

"Thank you, your Majesty."

"Don't mention it, Elliot. Furthermore, as a reward for your valor and effort in battle, I king Arthur, give you my eldest daughter, Athena in marriage. I can tell that your strong man and you have a lot of potential"

When the populace heard the declaration of the King. the girls who were lucky enough to avoid being captured, shrieked in excitement then sighed in disappointment.

At this moment, Athena walked up to me in a beautiful gown and I kissed her cherry red lips then and there. I was too mesmerized by her beauty to do anything else. Even though I met Lucy not that long ago, Athena was 1,000 times more beautiful than Lucy could ever be. Plus, Lucy is just a Commoner, while Athena is Royalty.

Afterward Mark and Mars were buried with all the honors of veteran knights. The whole populace of the Town of Beginnings was present at their funerals. I cried as they were buried. They were not only my teachers but also comrades after all.

Then the King of the Town of Beginnings made an announcement, "It is quite unfortunate that we had to sacrifice two veterans that were extremely talented. With that said, I would like to look forward towards a bright future. Elliot the son of the Mountain King step forward and kneel"

I did as I was told. The king took out his greatsword and said, "I, King Arthur the First, grant thee Elliot, the title of *The Hero of the Town of Beginnings*. Furthermore, because I have no sons of my own you are hereby officially named heir to the throne! Take care of this Town as well as my daughter, Athena, after my passing."

"I will! Thank you for your generosity, your Majesty! If I may be so bold as to ask for another request, your Majesty?"

"What is it, Elliot? You may speak freely"

"Now that I have accomplished great deeds, please allow me to go and see my father, the Mountain King."

"Of course! Take Athena with you, introduce her to your father. We are soon-to-be family after all."

"Of course!"

At that moment, a messenger rushed up to the King, "Urgent message your Majesty!"

"Speak!"

"Your daughter, the third princess has gone missing!"

"What! Guards! Guards!" yelled the King, panic in his voice. Once the guards had all gathered, he continued, "Investigate the whole town and search for the third princess!" "Sir, yes, sir!"

All the guards started investigating right away. Just like that, the Town of Beginnings was thrown into disarray once again.

CHAPTER 9

Heartbreak

Disclaimer: Lucy's point of view

Ever since I met Elliot, I couldn't stop thinking about him. I caught myself wanting to see him again. I have never felt this way about anyone before.

The town of Beginnings was attacked. I have heard from Mars that every spring the Barbarians would attack this town and steal supplies. I have noticed that most of the Barbarians are held back by our knights.

Then it happened. I heard stomps. Each stomp felt like an earthquake. I couldn't see what caused these "earthquakes", but I could tell that the creature was huge in size. After this creature showed up, the knights couldn't hold the frontline anymore.

After the Barbarians broke through, the Town of Beginnings lit on fire. Casualties started appearing everywhere. People were running in all directions. Their screams could be heard in the distance.

I noticed something. The Barbarians that broke through, some of them stole supplies, while others stole young girls my age. One of the Barbarians noticed me in a daze. Appearance wise he was a man with a round ugly face and a button nose. He was wearing armor and had his battle ax on his shoulder.

"Come here girly. I will take good care of you." After he said that he smiled creepily and I noticed that he had crooked teeth. I ran as fast as I could, but he was faster than me. I ran through many streets, but since the Barbarian was chasing me, I wasn't paying attention to where I was going and stumbled into a dead end.

"Finally cornered you. You are a tricky one, aren't ya? Now come here and stop resisting" He smiled creepily again. He was getting closer with every step, "Help!" When he heard me yell, he rushed at me to cover my mouth. He closed in on me and covered my mouth before I could call for help again.

"If you call for help again, I will kill you!" he threatened. At this point I was teary-eyed. The Barbarian noticed that I was on the verge of tears. He smiled to himself again and said, "I might as well enjoy your body while I am at it." I gasped with a terrified look on my face. The Barbarian pinned me down to the ground. I knew what he was about to do. I stopped resisting. I didn't see the point anymore. *I am sorry Elliot, I wanted to be yours alone. Now that dream is impossible.* With that I closed my eyes and waited for the pain to come. The pain never came.

When I opened my eyes again, the Barbarian that almost took my virginity lay on the ground next to me, his body sliced in half. I was covered in blood. When I looked up from the ground, I saw Mars with his greatsword in one hand, while the other one was extended towards me.

"Lucy, are you alright?" He said, "You are lucky that I made it just in time."

"I am fine thanks to you." I said while getting up and dusting myself off.

"Go to your room. Hide in the Military District until you hear the sound of Victory." With those words he disappeared into the streets. It was the last time I saw him.

I did as I was told and hid in my room in the Military District. A while later I heard cheers coming from the outside. I went to see what the commotion was all about.

As it turns out, Elliot has slain the creature that I saw a while back. Because of that, he has become a local celebrity. When the girls who were lucky enough not to get captured saw him, they shrieked with excitement and adoration in their eyes. I found myself getting annoyed and pouting whenever I heard their shrieks.

The King showed up. He wore traditional royal garments with a red cape. Then he called out Elliot and gave him the title of *The Hero of the Town Beginnings*.

Then I was heartbroken. Mars, the man who has rescued me, has perished in battle. The tears flowed like a river. Thankfully the King has agreed to bury Mars with honors. After the burial was completed, another tragedy struck. Athena, first princess and heir to the throne was given to Elliot as a wife. The worst part, he kissed her in front of everyone! That two-timer, good for nothing! I wish I hadn't fallen in love with such a man.

After that I don't remember much. I remember running away from Elliot as far as I could. Tears running down my face. That day my heartache doubled. It was the worst day of my life. I ended up running all the way to the Commoners' District. My childhood memories came back to me with new vigor.

There I saw a man. He was helping the poor and comforting them. He was lean. Not as handsome as Elliot though, and he didn't look strong at all. I greeted him saying, "Hello my name's Lucy, what's your name?"

When he heard me speak, he stopped what he was doing, turned around and said, "Nice to meet you Lucy, my name's Alejandro. Would you mind helping me feed these people? There's porridge right over there" he pointed towards the pot on the bonfire. I guess he made it himself. I nodded my head and did as I was told. We spent the rest of the day feeding the poor. Who knew that I would meet my future husband in the Commoners' District

CHAPTER 10

The Runaway

Disclaimer: Rose's point of view

I, the third princess, has decided to flee from the Town of Beginnings at the first sign of danger. Reason being my position to inherit the throne.

The Barbarians attacked. I could hear the swords clashing from the outside. I decided to run. My guess is that my father, the King, is too busy with the war effort. I couldn't find my sisters either.

I remembered my father telling us about an emergency passageway only known by the royal family. I gathered as much food and water [in a flask] as I could carry. I didn't even have time to change. Meanwhile, there were screams coming from the outside. It looks like the Barbarians broke through our defenses.

I made a run for it. I turned the corner and pulled on a lever, disguised as a lantern. The brick wall slid open revealing stairs going downward. I took the lantern on the wall and started going down the stairs. As far as I know the tunnel should lead straight to the outside.

After two hours of going down a straight I could finally see the light at the end of the tunnel. Before I exited the tunnel, I pulled a lever that activated the traps.

Once I exited the tunnel, I looked around to make sure that I really made it out. As it turns out, I appeared right outside the wooden wall. To not cross paths with any Barbarians I ran in the opposite direction.

Two days later. I ran out of food and water. I am exhausted from all the running. I ripped the lower half of my gown [to the point where my knees could be seen] because it was extremely uncomfortable to run in a gown. However, it was extremely embarrassing running like that. I felt as if I am half naked and losing my dignity as a princess.

On the third day, I felt as if I was going to die. I felt my consciousness fading. Before I fainted from exhaustion, I caught a glimpse of a village not too far away.

CHAPTER 11

Leo
The Master Merchant

Disclaimer: Leo's point of view

I, the second son of the Mountain King, have arrived in the Town of Beginnings. My father has told my brothers and I about the trial that we have to pass to become King.

Even though I am not as physically strong as Elliot, I can use my brain instead. The one I feel sorry for is Alejandro, he's the weakest of us all. All he does is listen to father's teachings every day.

When I arrived in the Town of Beginnings, I was mesmerized by it. I was especially drawn to the Noble District. There everyone was yelling at each other, haggling and selling their wares

One of the Merchants there saw me and called me over. He was a fat man with a round face and a round nose with dimples.

"What's your name kid?"

"Leo"

"Listen Leo. I am getting old. I am looking for an assistant. You see, my wife, God bless her, passed away. We were not blessed with children unfortunately."

"Why do you want me Mr. Merchant? Couldn't you have hired someone else?"

"You're right, I could have. However, most of them are older than you and don't learn as quickly. Also, you have driven and passion, I could see it in your eyes. What do you say? I will teach you everything you need to know." *This is my chance to develop myself!*

"Sure, I will take it!"

"That's what I am talking about! Let's go! My name's Marty. It's nice to meet you"

After a year of training, Marty has taught me many things. He taught me the rules of supply and demand, and how to use them most efficiently. However, most of all I love money! I love when there is a lot of it and I get to keep it all to myself.

The Barbarians attacked. The most heartbreaking thing is that the Barbarians stole more than half of the Town of Beginnings' supplies. That means, I lost a lot of money!

Then I was noticed by a group of Barbarians. One had a sword. Another had a shield. The third had a saber. The one with the sword chased after me, while the others killed all the merchants [including Master Marty] and stole the supplies.

The Barbarian with the sword chased me until I reached a dead end. I looked around to find a way to escape. There was none. I was already preparing myself for death, when I heard the slash of a sword.

As it turns out, the Barbarian with the sword was too focused on me to notice that someone was approaching him from behind. When I looked at the man who had saved my life, the man was holding a greatsword and had a muscular build. He said to me, "Hey kid, get out of here! It's too dangerous here!"

"Thank you, Mr.!"

"You must be extremely lucky. You're the second one I saved today. Now, go! I can't delay any longer!" With that the man left before I could say another word.

I found out the identity of my Savior, Mars, the commander of the knights. Last I heard he perished in the battle against the Barbarians. Sad. if it wasn't for him, I would be dead.

I attended his funeral to pay my respects. Then I heard something that shocked me. It turns out that Elliot, my older brother, was the MVP of the battlefield. He has received the honorary title of *The Hero of the Town of Beginnings,* as well as the first princess, Athena as his wife, by extension making him the heir to the throne of the Town of Beginnings. I am very jealous of him.

To not fall behind my brother in terms of achievements, I started building my own Merchant Empire. Because all the merchants were killed by the Barbarians, I was able to monopolize every trade imaginable in the Town of Beginnings. I hired many apprentices that were capable and built my Empire fairly quickly. I sold the goods cheaply and became rich very fast. It was easy because of the lack of competition.

Using my influence, I restocked the lost supplies and bought many treasures. I will use these treasures to show my father what I have accomplished.

I got married. The woman that I chose to marry was one of my apprentices that I hired. She was the most capable, only second to me. She was as passionate about money as I am.

Now I have everything. I have money. I have a wife. I can go to my father and show him what I have accomplished.

CHAPTER 12

Alejandro
The Commoner

Disclaimer: Alejandro's point of view

When my father, the Mountain King, gave Elliot, Leo and I, a trial to develop ourselves and explore the world while keeping his commandments, I took it to heart.

When I arrived in the Town of Beginnings, I explored all three Districts. What surprised me the most, is the fact that the Church District combined with the Commoner District are the least visited places.

After exploring all three Districts, I visited the Church in the middle of the Church District. There, I was greeted by the Pope, "Hello my son, what can I do for you today?"

"Hello Holy Father, I was wondering if there is anything I can do to help around here?"

"As a matter of fact, there is one thing. Take these pieces of cloth and deliver them to the poor in the Commoner's District."

"All right! Thank you, Holy Father!"

I did as I was told. Indeed, there were many people who were shivering. I gave people the pieces of cloth and went back to the Church. I continued to work with the Church to help the commoners in the Commoner's District. I would cook for them, bring them more clothes and medicine, among other things.

The Barbarians attacked the Town of Beginnings. I heard from the Pope that they attack every Spring to get supplies for the upcoming Winter. Screams could be heard everywhere.

Thanks to the quick thinking of the Pope, we were able to hide most of the Commoners. We hid in the Church. Thankfully the Barbarians didn't find us since they were interested in the supplies, the majority of which were located in the Noble's District.

After the Barbarian attack was repelled by the knights, word got around that two veterans, along with 200 knights perished during the battle.

Furthermore, one knight who has performed exceptionally well. So well in fact, that he was given the title *The Hero of the Town of Beginnings*. It turns out that knight is my eldest brother, Elliot. In addition, he was betrothed to the first princess of the Town of Beginnings. I was extremely happy for him.

That same day, as I was feeding the Commoners the porridge that I cooked for them [as was the custom], a girl came up to me and asked, "Do you need any help?"

I answered saying, "Yea, help me feed these people. See that pot over there?" I pointed towards the pot standing on the bonfire, "Grab the porridge and feed the people" I found out that the girl's name is Lucy.

We continued to help the commoners in the Commoner's District. Lucy told me a lot of things: She told me she used to live in the Commoner's District, how Mars raised and saved her from a Barbarian. Finally, she told me about Elliot and how heartbroken she was because of him.

Time passed. Lucy and I got married at the Church that we often helped out in. We invited many to our wedding. After the wedding, I decided to visit my father, the Mountain King.

However, I did not know what to say to him. Elliot became a Hero of the Town of Beginnings. Leo, I heard that he became a wealthy Merchant with an established trade network. What about me? I have nothing. I accomplished nothing.

After thinking for a while, I have decided. I will tell my father and apologize to him for not achieving great deeds. With my mind made up, I headed towards the mountains with my wife in tow.

Epilogue

Two years have passed since the day that Elliot, Leo and Alejando have left their father, the Mountain King to go explore the world.

Elliot, the firstborn has returned saying, "Look father, I am a Hero of the Town of Beginnings. My wife is the first princess. I have glory and power combined! This is the true meaning of life."

The Mountain King replied to him saying, "Your hands are stained with blood. Your desire for power and glory has corrupted your soul. You are not worthy to become King"

The second son Leo, brought many treasures saying, "Look father, I have the whole world in my grasp. I can buy and sell many wares, turning the tears of many into silver and success."

The Mountain King replied to him saying, "You are very similar to your brother, Elliot. The both of you have traded in the treasures of the soul for something else. Elliot traded it in for glory and power, while you traded it in for gold. The both of you are not worthy."

The third son Alejandro, fell to his knees saying, "Forgive me father. I have not achieved anything noteworthy. I humbled myself. Forgave my enemies."

The Mountain King answered him with warmth in his voice saying, "Your soul is pure and filled with goodness. So, what if you didn't gain fame or riches. You have kept my commandments. I give my throne to you."

When Elliot heard this, he was furious at first. However, he said to himself, *I don't need the throne, I am guaranteed to be the Lord of the Town of begins.*

When Leo heard what father had decided, he was even more furious than Elliot. He said to himself, *I understand why Elliot isn't very upset. He has become the Hero of the Town of Beginnings. In addition, he is betrothed to the first princess. But why Alejandro? He is the weakest of us all! I should be King, not him! I swear Alejandro, I shall have my revenge!*

After Alejandro was pronounced King, a feast was organized for the new King and a crown was placed on top of his head.

Afterword

I appreciate you reading and purchasing my new book. Also, please keep in mind that the more copies you guys buy, the sooner I can publish my next book, which is also a romance novel called "I wish".

For me, this is a new genre. I'm hoping you will appreciate the plot and the personality of each character in it. I left this book with a few cliffhangers unfinished. The possibility of a story continuation is the reason.

If you enjoyed what you read, let me know. I may then decide whether to continue the story after that. Your truthful comments are appreciated so, you can reach me at my socials below:

Email: zubinbviktor@yahoo.com

Website: VZAnimationWorld.com

YouTube: Vaminationz

www.ingramcontent.com/pod-product-compliance
Lightning Source LLC
LaVergne TN
LVHW012103070526
838200LV00073BA/3411